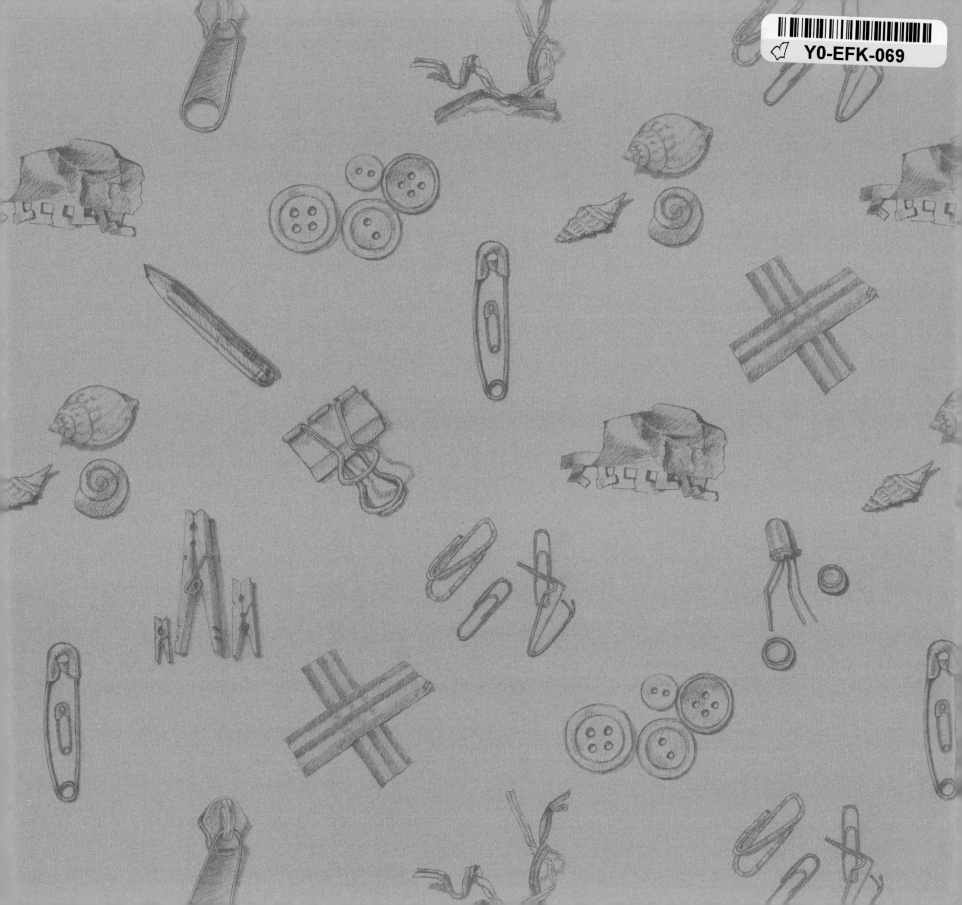

For Tim

Lonely Bird

Ruth Whiting

CANDLEWICK PRESS

Lonely Bird is an artist and very fond of the family she lives with. She is also rather shy, so she prefers to watch them from a safe distance.

"Do you think they even know I am here?"

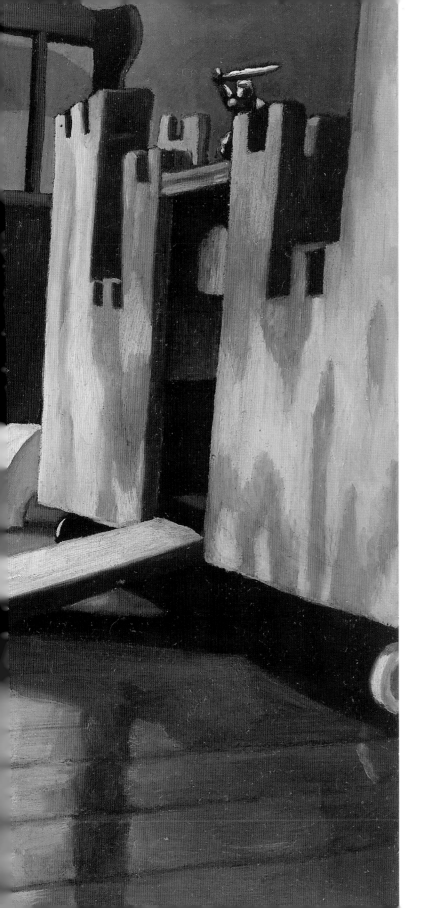

Like her, the smallest family member likes to make things.

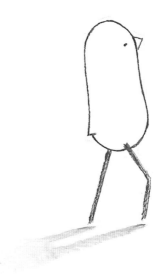

When Lonely Bird needs inspiration for her art, she ventures out to explore.

Books are always a good place to start. The most inspiring books are the ones with lots of pictures.

Her head full of ideas, Lonely Bird is now ready to go collecting.

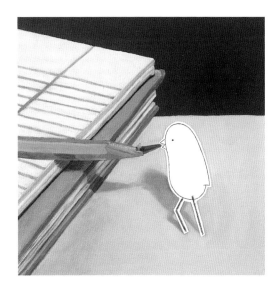
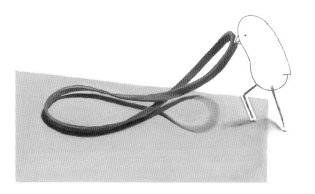

Lonely Bird carries her treasure home.
Outside her door she finds . . . a visitor?
  "Hello. You look like you could use a
friend and a bit of cheering up. Follow me."

Lonely Bird leads her crumpled guest
into the narrow space behind the green
bookshelf.
  "Welcome to my home. Let's see if I have
anything that might help you feel better."

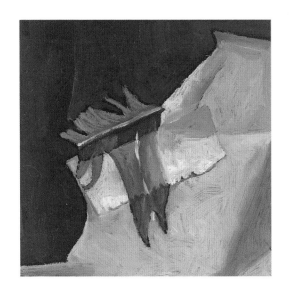

"Does that tickle?"   "Try to hold still."   "Almost done."

"There, now you look more like yourself."

"In fact I'd say you look ready for an adventure!"

Then Lonely Bird hears a familiar noise, a dreadful noise, a horrible, roaring, sucking noise.
"Quick, follow me!"

For a few moments, Lonely Bird can't move or think.

Finally, she knows what she must do. She waits for night to fall.

When the house is still and dark, Lonely Bird sets out to rescue her friend.

Crossing the kitchen seems to take forever.

At last, she reaches the monster's lair. She enters.

The beast lies quietly in the gloom. Lonely Bird will need a light.

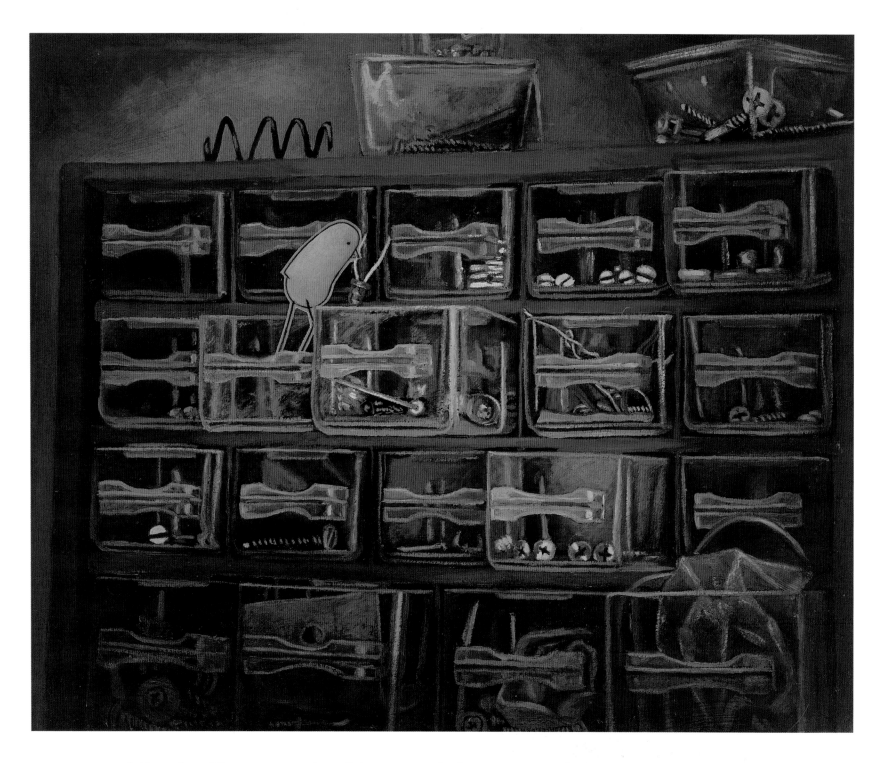

Luckily, she likes to make things, and the monster's lair is a warehouse of useful materials.

Now Lonely Bird is ready. Into the sleeping monster's throat she goes.

"There you are. Let's get you home."

"Up you go."

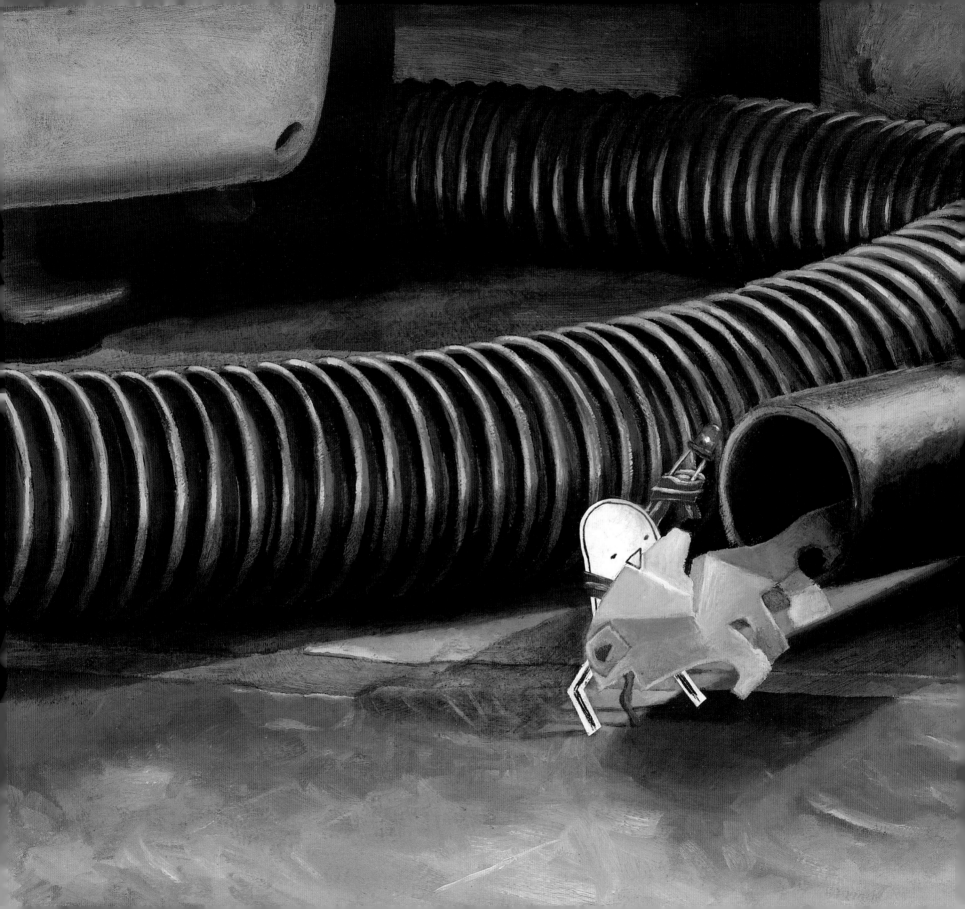

At last the friends struggle free.

In the dawn light, Lonely Bird sees that her friend is injured.

"A little patching up will help you feel better."

She brings him to the place
with the best supplies: a sunny
place of busy making.

Oh, look. A perfect habitat.

Lonely Bird gets to work.

There! He looks right at home.

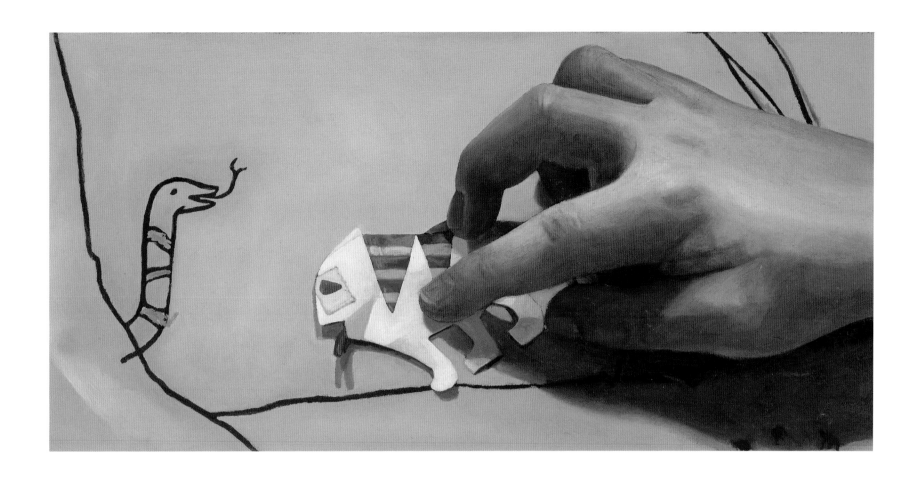

The small one awakes and finds the new friend.

"I will call you Wigglet," she says. "Would you like me to draw you a fly to catch, Wigglet? You look hungry."

Lonely Bird smiles. She hadn't known her friend's name.

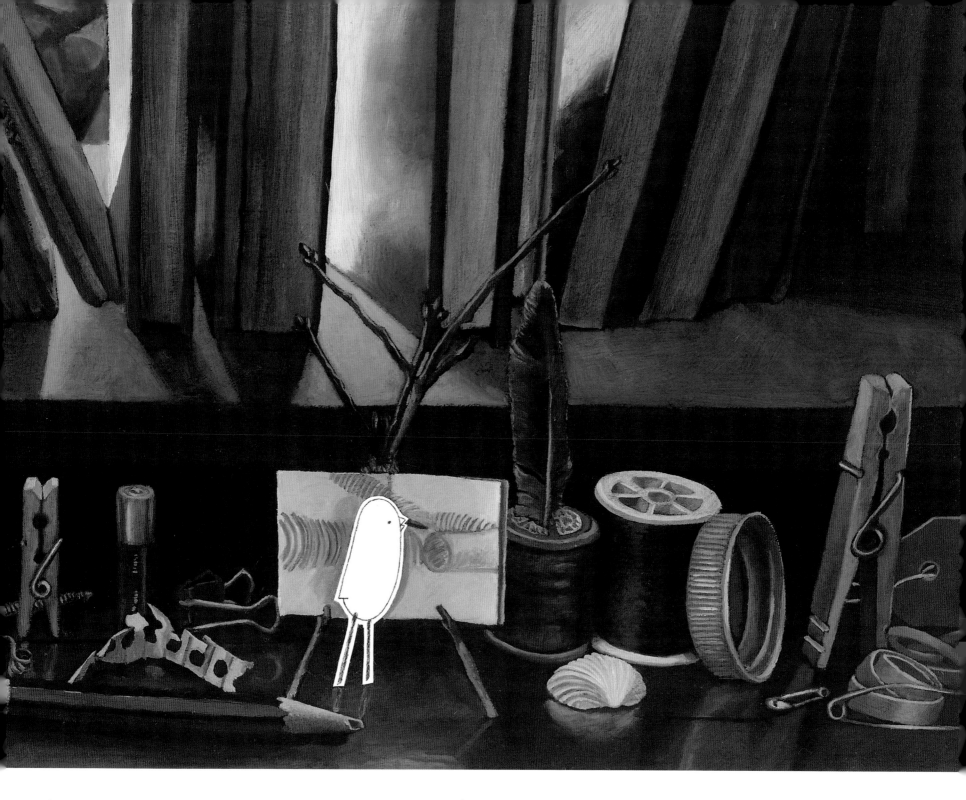

Back home in the narrow space behind the green bookshelf,
Lonely Bird creates something new.

And she knows just who to share it with.

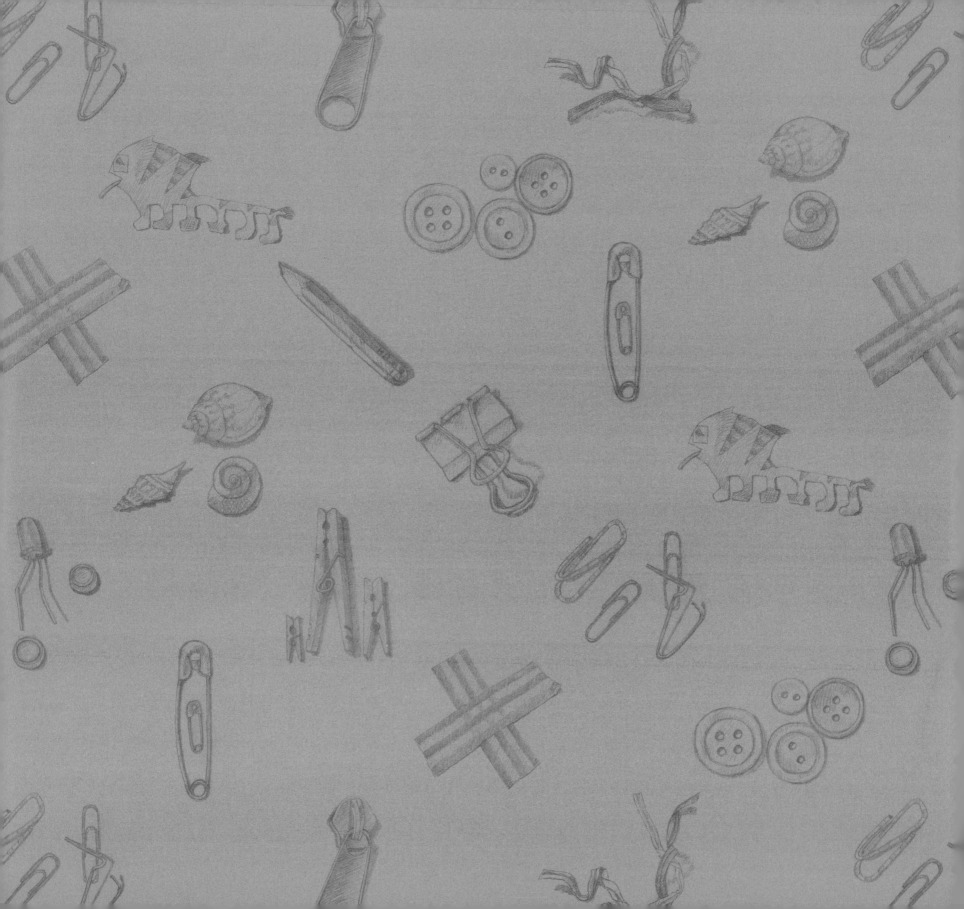